Little T
and the
Dragon's Tooth

written and illustrated by
Frank Rodgers

PICTURE WINDOW BOOKS
Minneapolis, Minnesota

Editor: Nick Healy
Page Production: Brandie E. Shoemaker
Creative Director: Keith Griffin
Editorial Director: Carol Jones

First American edition published in 2007 by
Picture Window Books
5115 Excelsior Boulevard
Suite 232
Minneapolis, MN 55416
877-845-8392
www.picturewindowbooks.com

First published in 2002 by A&C Black Publishers Limited, 38 Soho Square,
London W1D 3HB, with the title THE DRAGON'S TOOTH.

Printed in the United States of America.

Library of Congress Cataloging-in-Publication Data
Rodgers, Frank, 1944-
Little T and the dragon's tooth / by Frank Rodgers.— 1st American ed.
p. cm. — (Read-it! chapter books)
Summary: On Dragon Day, Little T and his friends try to scare everyone else
by pretending a real dragon is nearby, and when they discover they were right,
the only way to save the castle is to lure another dragon there.
ISBN-13: 978-1-4048-2727-1 (hardcover)
ISBN-10: 1-4048-2727-7 (hardcover)
[1. Festivals—Fiction. 2. Dragons—Fiction. 3. Lost children—Fiction.
4. Tyrannosaurus rex—Fiction. 5. Dinosaurs—Fiction.] I. Title. II. Series.
PZ7.R6154Litd 2007
[E]—dc22   2006003419

Table of Contents

Chapter One

Little Prince T Rex was busy. He was making a big dragon head for Dragon Day.

His mom and dad, Queen Teena Regina and King High T the Mighty, were trying on funny dragon hats.

The dinosaurs were putting on funny
dragon costumes.

Everyone loved Dragon Day. It
gave them a chance to dress up and
have fun.

"Why do we have Dragon Day, Mom?" asked Little T.

Queen Teena said, "Long ago, a dragon with a bad temper came to the castle.

"He stole your great-grandmother, Princess Rexeen, and wouldn't give her back."

"What happened?" asked Little T.

"Your great-grandfather, Prince Capital T, disguised himself as a dragon and went to rescue her," said Queen Teena.

"How?" asked Little T.

"Yes," said his mom with a grin.
"Dragon jokes."

"He laughed so much that the
prince escaped with the princess,"
said the queen.

"From that day on, the dinosaurs have celebrated her rescue by holding a Dragon Day," she added. "They dress up as dragons and tell dragon jokes."

The costumes are meant to be funny and make the dinosaurs laugh.

Mine won't! It's going to be scary! My friends are going to help me.

Chapter Two

Little T's friends Don, Bron, Tops, and Dinah were waiting for him at the castle gates.

They had made a wonderful body for the dragon.

Now we can put on the costume and give everyone a scare!

Little T lifted the dragon's head over Tops, while Don, Bron, and Dinah got under the dragon's body.

Cool!

"I'll go and tell the dinosaurs there's a real dragon coming," said Little T.

They'll be surprised.

13

The dinosaurs were surprised.

Little T ran toward them shouting,
"Look out! Look out!"

As the dragon charged toward them,
the dinosaurs started to run away.

But they soon stopped.

The "real" dragon
had tripped over
its tail,

fallen in
a heap,

and lost
its head.

"Ha-ha!" laughed the dinosaurs.
"That's the funniest 'real' dragon
ever! Well done, Little T!"

Little T glared. It wasn't supposed to be funny. The dragon was supposed to scare the dinosaurs.

Fed up, he and his friends trudged back to the castle.

Suddenly, Little T noticed something on the ground.

He picked it up.

"What's this?" he said.

"It looks like a little elephant's tusk," said Don.

"Can't be," said Dinah. "There are no elephants around here."

Maybe it's a piece of a toy.

Little T grinned. "Let's pretend it's a dragon's tooth," he said. "We can make big footprints and show them to the dinosaurs."

They went to the edge of the forest, where the ground was soft, and got to work.

They stamped shapes that looked like a dragon's footprints in the mud.

"Now for the pretend dragon's tooth," said Little T with a grin. He dropped it beside the footprints.

Little T then rushed off to warn
the dinosaurs that there was a huge
dragon around. He had the proof.

The dinosaurs didn't really believe
him, but they came to look anyway.
They thought it might turn out to be
funny again.

"There!" said Little T, pointing to the footprints and the pretend dragon's tooth.

The dinosaurs looked down.

Then they looked up into the forest.
"You're right!" they cried in panic.

There is a dragon! Run!

All the dinosaurs suddenly turned
and ran for their lives.

Chapter Three

Little T and his friends laughed.

"We scared them after all," said
Little T.

They were surprised!

But now it was Little T and his
friends' turn to be surprised. They
heard a loud sound behind them.

WAAAAAR!

A dragon came out of the forest.

Everyone stood
frozen with fear.

Little T gasped and
looked down at the
pretend dragon's tooth. "It was real
after all," he whispered.

24

At that moment, Little T's mom and dad came running up.

"Don't worry! I'll save you!" cried High T.

But he slipped on the muddy ground and fell onto his face.

"WAAAR!" cried the dragon again.

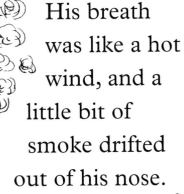 His breath was like a hot wind, and a little bit of smoke drifted out of his nose.

Queen Teena skidded to a halt in front of the dragon.

"Be careful, Mom!" cried Little T.

He might roast you!

But Queen Teena smiled and picked up the tooth.

"I don't think so," she said. "He's just a baby! This is one of his baby teeth."

My guess is that he's lost and he's looking for his mother.

"WAAAR!" wailed the baby dragon. His big, warm tears dropped onto High T's head.

The king sighed as he washed away the mud.

Just like a hot shower!

27

Queen Teena took the baby dragon's hand. "Let's all go back and tell the dinosaurs," the queen said.

The dinosaurs were glad that the dragon was only a baby. But they were worried that his mom would have a bad temper like the dragon who stole the princess long ago.

"But we must find her," said Queen Teena.

A baby needs his mother.

The dinosaurs sighed and agreed.

You're right, but how can we find her?

Chapter Four

Suddenly Little T had an idea. "Baby dragons can't fly," he said. "But their moms can. We should put something into the sky to attract her attention."

She might be flying around nearby.

"Like what?" asked his dad.

"A dragon," replied Little T, pointing to the dragon costume.

"How will you get that into the sky?"
asked his dad.

We can't do magic,
and the royal magician
is on vacation.

"We don't need magic," Little T said.

We need hot
air to make
it rise like
a balloon.

"Where on Earth will we get hot air?" asked High T.

Queen Teena smiled. "From the baby dragon, of course," she said. "Isn't that right, Little T?"

Little T quickly tied the pieces of the costume together with a long rope.

Then he showed the baby dragon
what he wanted him to do.

"Like this!" he said.
His friends lifted
up the costume,
and Little T blew
into the head.

The baby dragon thought it was a
game and smiled.

"WAAAR!" he cried and, copying
Little T, he blew a long blast of hot
air into the head.

The dragon costume slowly rose into the sky.

Wonderful!

But as the dragon costume bobbed high in the air, the dinosaurs began to get worried.

But before they could do anything,
there was a great rushing noise.

A huge dragon swooped down from the sky above.

WHOOSH!

It was the baby dragon's mother.

Flames curled out of
her nose, and her
breath was as hot as
a furnace.

She looked around quickly. When she
spotted the other dragon, she threw
out her arms. "Babykins!" she cried.

Come to
Mommy!

The baby dragon
leaped into his
mother's arms,
and she gave
him a big hug.

Chapter Five

The dinosaurs sighed. "Ahhh," they murmured.

Then they realized they were still wearing their silly dragon costumes.

Slowly, they began to back away.

"Wait a moment," said the big
dragon. "Don't go. I haven't had
a chance to look at all your lovely
costumes yet."

I think they're very funny!

You do?

"Of course," replied the mother
dragon. "I love funny things."

"Oh yes," replied the baby dragon's mother. "My grandfather used to tell me lots. It seems that a funny little dragon once made him laugh so much that it cured his bad temper."

Now all dragons tell jokes!

"Well," said Queen Teena, "you've certainly come to the right place for jokes."

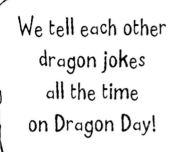

We tell each other dragon jokes all the time on Dragon Day!

"Super!" cried the mother dragon.
"Let me tell you one!"

Why is a dragon like the weather in the desert?

We don't know!

"Because it's always a scorcher!"
cried the big dragon. She threw her
head back and bellowed
with laughter.

"Ha-ha!" she roared. Flames shot out of her nose and into the sky. "A scorcher. Get it?"

"We do," said the dinosaurs, grinning. "Now it's our turn."

Why did the dragon sit on the tomato?

The mother dragon smiled and said, "I don't know."

"It wanted to play squash!" said the dinosaur. Once more, the dragon roared with laughter.

"This is the most fun ever!" she cried. "Babykins and I are going to come here every year!"

Aren't we, Babykins?

The baby dragon was playing with Little T's younger sister.

"WAAAR!" he cried, smiling and nodding.

The dinosaurs were delighted. "We'll have real dragons for Dragon Day!" they cried.

Thanks to you and your friends, Little T!

Little T grinned. "It won't be scary, though, will it?" he said.

I liked it when we were being scary.

He turned to his friends.

Maybe next year we should look for a monster or a ghost to invite to Dragon Day.

"Great idea!" cried his friends.

"Ha!" snorted the dinosaurs.

But Little T just smiled. "Oh, no?"
he said. "Just wait and see."

Look for More *Read-it!* Chapter Books

Looking for a specific title? A complete list
of *Read-it!* Chapter Books is available on our Web site:
www.picturewindowbooks.com